the surprise garden

by **zoe hall**

illustrated by **shari halpern**

The Blue Sky Press · An Imprint of Scholastic Inc. · New York

THE BLUE SKY PRESS

Text copyright © 1998 by Zoe Hall
Illustrations copyright © 1998 by Shari Halpern

Special thanks to Ted Maclin, Coordinator of the Children's Garden program
at the Brooklyn Botanic Garden, for his expert advice on gardening.

Library of Congress Cataloging-in-Publication Data
Hall, Zoe, 1957-
The surprise garden / by Zoe Hall ; illustrated by Shari Halpern.
— 1st ed.   p.   cm.
Summary: After sowing unmarked seeds, three youngsters
wait expectantly for their garden to grow.
ISBN 0-590-10075-0
[1. Gardens—Fiction. 2. Seeds—Fiction. 3. Vegetables—Fiction.]
I. Halpern, Shari, ill. II. Title.
PZ7.H1528Su   1998   [E]—DC21   97-9735   CIP   AC
10 9 8 7 6 5 4 3 2 1   8 9/9 0/0 01 02 03
Printed in the United States of America   37
First printing, February 1998
Art direction by Kathleen Westray
Designed by Kristina Iulo

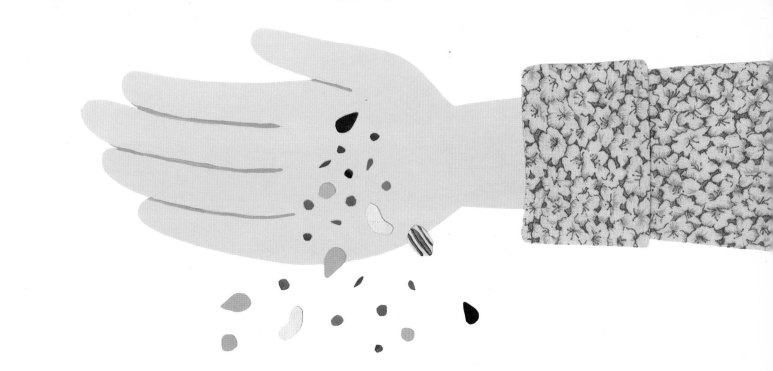

We're planting the seeds for a surprise garden.
Can you guess what we will grow?

We don't know.
It's a SURPRISE!

First, we use our trowel and rake
to loosen the soil.

Mom has given us each a handful
of all kinds of seeds.
Look at all the different shapes and sizes!

We poke the seeds into the soil,
one by one.
We have painted sticks different colors
to mark the different kinds of seeds.

Then we water the seeds
and wait for our surprise garden to grow.

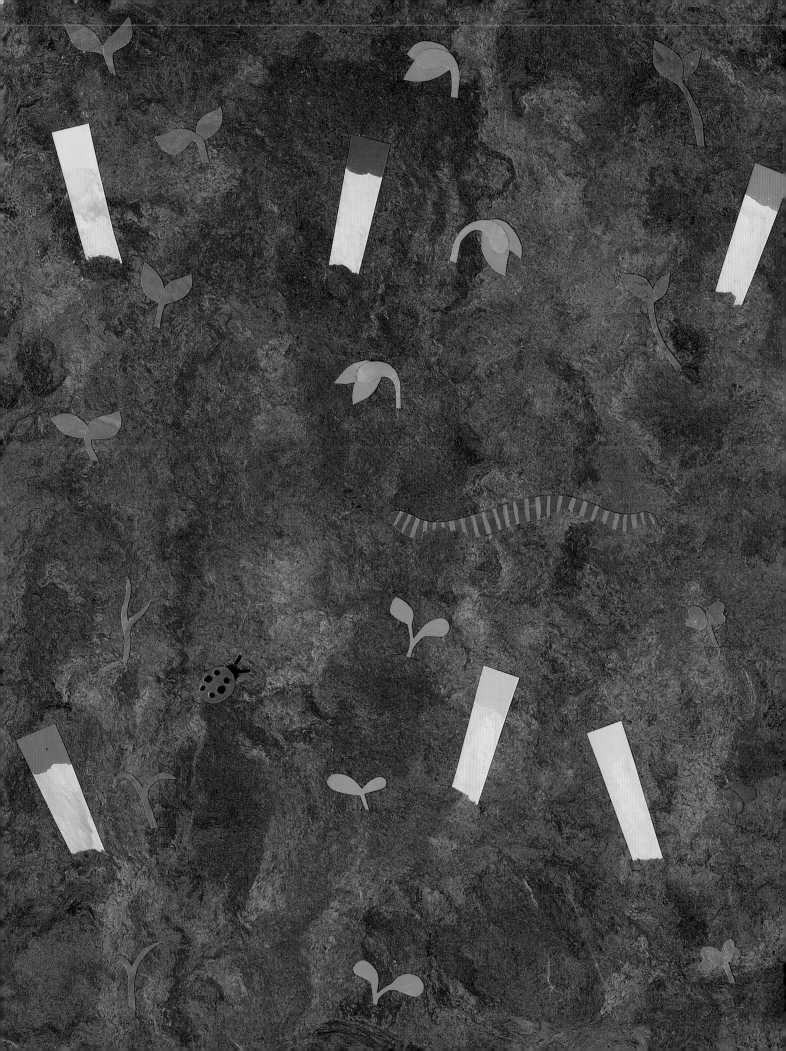

Soon, the seeds sprout into small green shoots.

We water the plants,
and the sun warms them.
Our garden grows and grows!
On some plants, flowers bloom.

Before long, the petals fall off.
SURPRISE!
We see peas, beans, and squash.

On some plants,
leaves grow close to the ground.
SURPRISE!
We see spinach and lettuce.

And what is growing here?
SURPRISE!
We see broccoli and cauliflower.

Is anything growing here?
SURPRISE!
We find carrots and radishes.
They are growing under the ground.

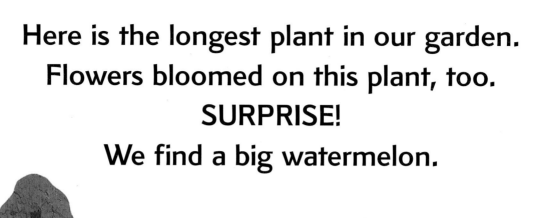

Here is the longest plant in our garden.
Flowers bloomed on this plant, too.
SURPRISE!
We find a big watermelon.

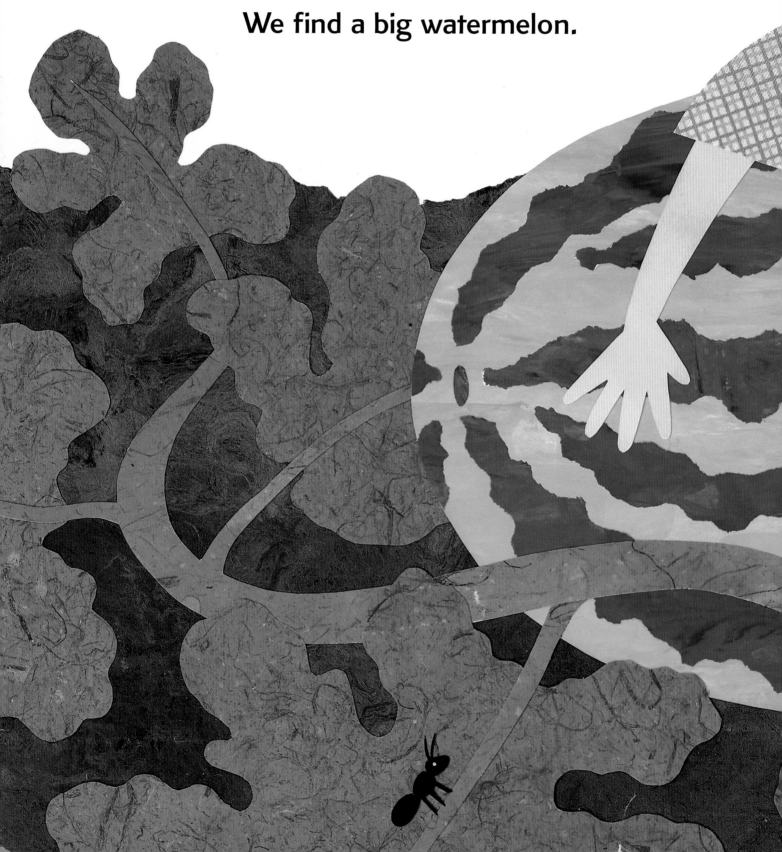

Here is the tallest plant in our garden.
SURPRISE!
It's a sunflower, and it is full of tasty seeds.

All summer long,
the food in our surprise garden ripens.
We like to pick the food. . .

. . . and eat it, too!
SURPRISE!
We're having a garden party!

What we grew in our surprise garden:

These seeds grew into **pea** and **bean** plants. We eat the seeds, and sometimes the pods, of these plants.

These tiny seeds grew into **spinach** and **lettuce** plants. The leaves are good to eat.

These small seeds grew into **broccoli** and **cauliflower** plants. The parts we eat are really the flower buds.

These tiny seeds grew into **carrot** and **radish** plants. We eat the roots that grow underground.

These seeds grew into **squash** and **watermelon** plants. We eat these plants' fruits.

This striped seed grew into a tall **sunflower** plant. We eat the seeds of the flower.

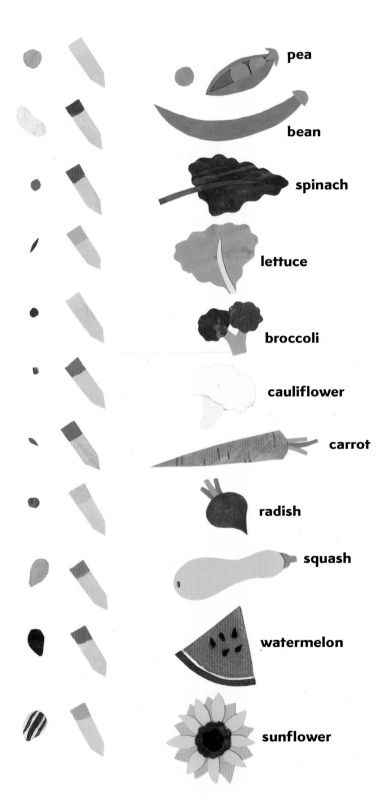

pea

bean

spinach

lettuce

broccoli

cauliflower

carrot

radish

squash

watermelon

sunflower